SUPERDAISY

For SuperDaisy, brave and inspiring ~ R. S.

For all the little superheroes ~ Z. W.

The Little Princess Trust provides free, real-hair wigs for
young cancer sufferers and for children and young people experiencing
the devastating effects of hair loss. They also fund pioneering, life-saving
research into childhood cancers. Established in 2006, the Little Princess Trust
has supplied over 12,000 wigs to children and young people and invested
nearly £15 million into ground-breaking childhood cancer research.
If you would like to find out more, please visit www.littleprincesses.org.uk.

First published in paperback by HarperCollins *Children's Books* in 2022

1 3 5 7 9 10 8 6 4 2

ISBN: 978-0-00-847068-5

HarperCollins *Children's Books* is a division of HarperCollins*Publishers* Ltd
1 London Bridge Street, London SE1 9GF

www.harpercollins.co.uk

HarperCollins*Publishers*, 1st Floor, Watermarque Building,
Ringsend Road, Dublin 4, Ireland

Printed in Great Britain by Bell and Bain Ltd, Glasgow

SUPERDAISY

REBECCA SMITH

ILLUSTRATED BY
ZOE WARING

HarperCollins *Children's Books*

Think of a princess . . . imagine her there,
with thick golden locks and a high golden chair.

Daisy – the **SWEETEST**,

most **LOVELY** of girls,

dreamed of cascading,

PRINCESS-LIKE CURLS.

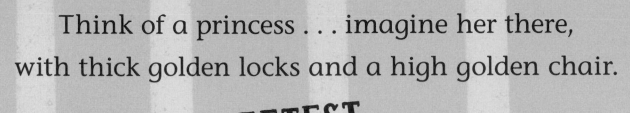

And if you asked Daisy
then she would confess,
she **LOVED** dressing up
like a fairy princess.

There in
the costume box
under her bed,
she kept a **PINK GOWN**
and a crown for
her head.

She'd put on her crown and her **FABULOUS** dress,

and – **TA-DA!** – there she'd be:

a **FAIRY PRINCESS!**

And while she was playing she would not have to think
about things not so happy nor sparkly and pink . . .

. . . about visiting hospital, far from her home
and the times she felt poorly, sad and alone.
See, Daisy took medicine that made her feel bad
to help her get rid of the cancer she had.

At times she felt so very ill and so weak,
it was almost too much to smile or to speak.
But, worst of the lot, what felt MOST UNFAIR:
the medicine made Daisy lose all of her hair!

Her locks fell out
when they came
to be brushed.

And her
PRINCESS DREAMS
felt terribly crushed.

A crackle of magic, and out of the blue
our Daisy found herself at the **TOWN ZOO!**

RACOONS

LEMURS

ZOO

TICKETS

FEEDING TIMES

CAPYBARA   - 11.30
RACOONS   - 12.00
OTTERS   - 12.00
LEMURS   - 12.30
MEERKATS   - 13.00
MINIBEASTS - 14.00
           - 14.30

CAPYBARA
MONKEYS
MINIBEASTS
RACOONS
MEERKATS

Please do not feed us.

Please do not feed us.

"Five, four, three, two, one, zero, somebody must need a **SUPERHERO!**"

YES! The lemurs were making a terrible din . . .
A boy stood shaking their tree with a grin.
He laughed at their fear as they clutched at small twigs,
then Daisy strode up in her **FABULOUS** wig.

"Excuse me," she said. "You are being **UNKIND**.
Read the sign here, and I think you will find

kindness and care is the number-one rule!
Cruelty to animals is **REALLY** uncool."

The boy stopped shaking the lemurs' tall tree.
His cheeks burned with **SHAME** almost instantly.

"You're right," he said, "that was just mean and unfair.
But can I say – you have **SUCH COOL** hero hair!"

PLEASE BE
KIND TO THE
🐾 ANIMALS! 🐾

That week on the ward, Daisy wore her pink hair.

It gave her the **POWER** to fight things that **WEREN'T FAIR.**

And when she felt ill or unhappy or low
she'd smile, knowing she was a SUPERHERO!

The next time it happened, our Daisy was **READY!**
A **CRACKLE**, a **FLASH** – she held herself steady.

Then – "Five, four, three, two, one, zero, somebody must need a **SUPERHERO!**"

YES! Trapped in a wood,
a bear grunted and groaned.

"My scratching tree fell on me!
PLEASE HELP!"
he moaned.

Daisy summoned her strength
and HEAVED at the tree.
Up it came with a creak —
the bear was SET FREE!

They soon found a **NEW TREE**,
as good as before.

The bear scratched his back

and gave a glad
ROAR!

Daisy smiled, flicking her **PINK HERO HAIR**, so **PROUD** she could help a bear in despair!

That week on the ward,
Daisy wore her **PINK** hair.
It gave her the **POWER** to
fight things that weren't fair.
And when she felt ill
or unhappy or low
she'd smile, knowing she
was a **SUPERHERO!**

In the car,
singing **LOUD**
to her
FAVOURITE band,

Daisy suddenly found she was **STANDING ON SAND!**

A flash, a crackle – "Five, four, three, two, one, zero, somebody must need a **SUPERHERO!**"

YES! A girl stared at her ice cream, A-SPLAT on the sand.
Daisy came up beside her and took her small hand.
"That seagull," the girl sobbed, "came close and I SCREAMED.

It scared me and I dropped
my FAVOURITE ice creeeeam!"

Daisy looked that seagull
in its beady eyes.
"You **MEAN**, naughty birdie,
to make this girl **CRY!**

You know that you gave her a
FRIGHT and a **SCARE**,
now she's dropped her ice cream:
it's double unfair!"

The seagull and Daisy went back to the van.
It nodded with guilt as she spoke to the man.

Then she followed its lead across the white sand,
a **BRIGHT PINK** ice cream firmly clutched in each hand.

"Thank you," the girl said. "It's so nice that you care,

and please can I try on your
PINK HERO HAIR?"

Now the medicine is all put away,
Daisy is **BETTER** and ready to play,
but deep inside she will always be
A SUPERHERO – just watch and see.

Her strength, her smile, one cheeky wink –
and Daisy's golden locks flash pink!